橘メアリー
Tachibana MARY

蜜ぱら

Tachibana MARY

FIRST PHOTO BOOK
Location in Thailand

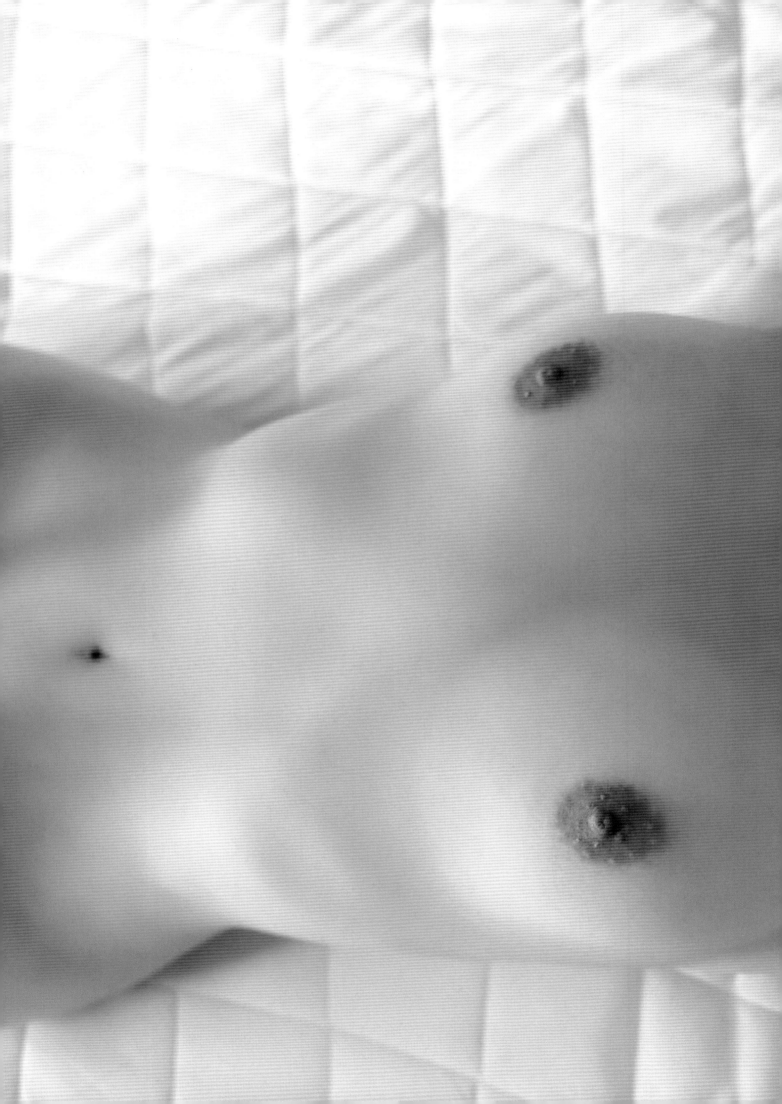

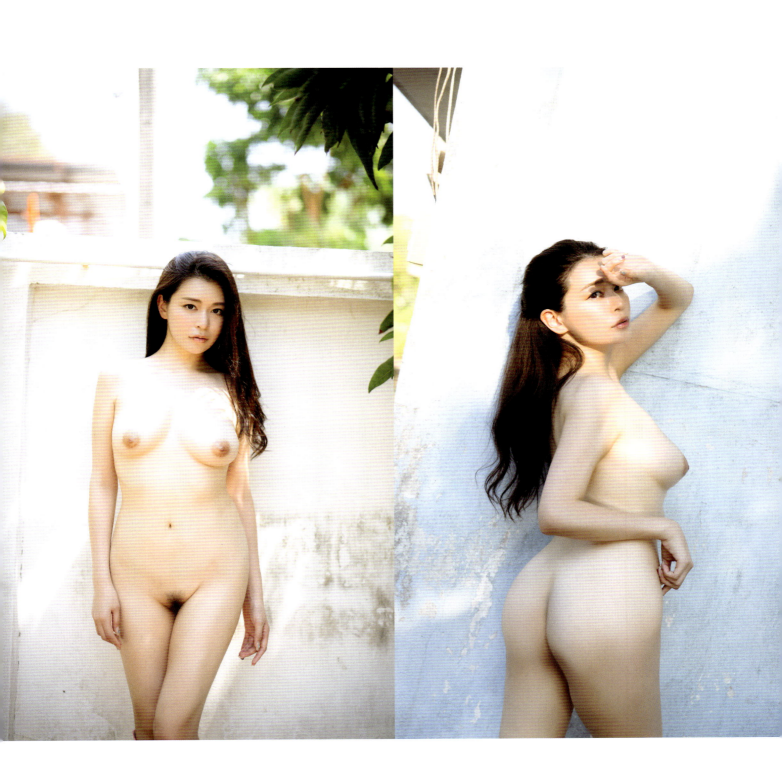

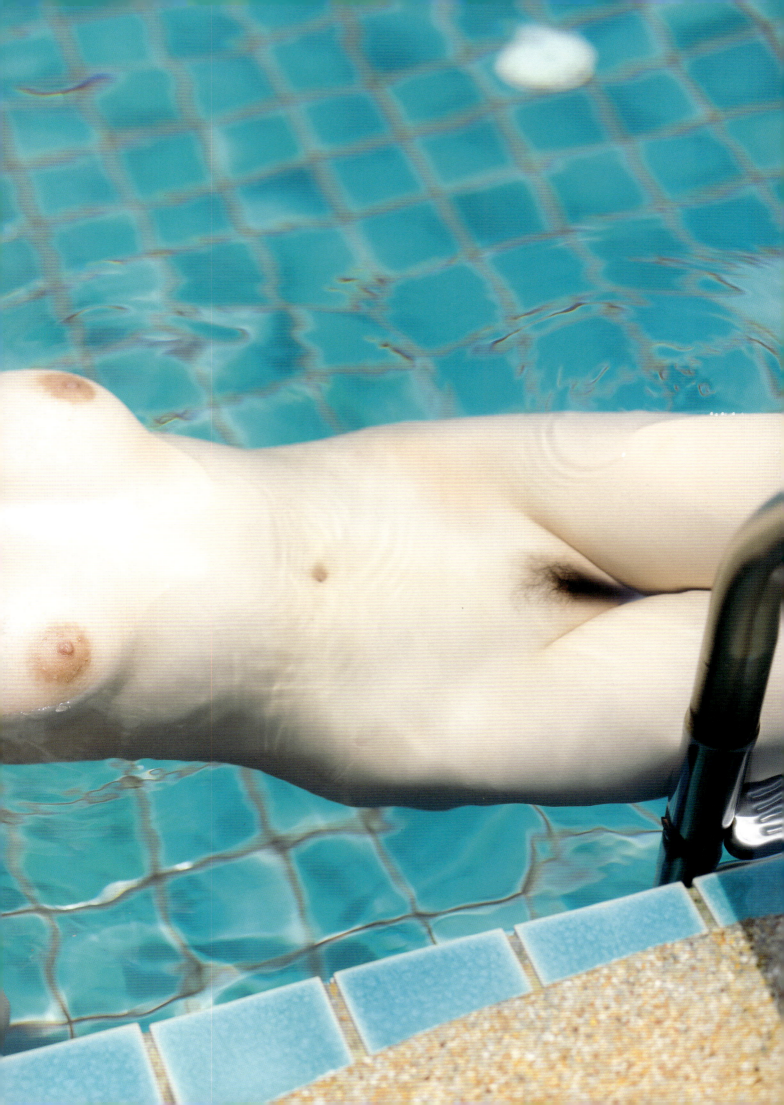

Tachibana MARY
FIRST PHOTO BOOK
Location in Thailand

Artist: TACHIBANA MARY
Photographer: MAKIHARA SUSUMU
Styling: TACHIBANA MARY
　　　　TOSHIKUNI ISAKO
Hair and make-up: TOSHIKUNI ISAKO
Artist Managemen: OKAMOTO KANA (LIGHT)
　　　　　　　　　TADA AKARI (LIGHT)
Art Director: MIZUKI RYOTA
Editor: SHIBATA HIROSHI (TAKESHOBO)

本書の無断複写・複製・転載を禁じます。定価はカバーに表記してあります。
乱丁・落丁があった場合は　furyo@takeshobo.co.jp　までメールにてお問い合わせください。

©2024 Takeshobo Co.,Ltd.